This book belongs to

· ·

Wiggleson is busy making treats for all his friends.

He wants to let his friends know how much he loves them and the reasons why.

He loves Prickles because she is so much fun.

They always play hide-and-seek together.

He loves Morris because he is very creative.

He makes lovely warm socks for Wiggleson.

He Loves Bugzy
because she is
super intelligent.

She was already
reading Charles
Dickens at age 3!

He loves Coco because he is so calm, cool, and collected.

He is the perfect cat to chill out with when you need relaxation time.

He loves Lilly because she is patient.

(Even when her little brothers and sisters are naughty)

He loves Nigel because he is adventurous.

He is always up to something new and exciting.

Wiggleson is tired after making all the cakes for his friends.

He takes a nap while he waits for them.

He hears his friends approaching and jumps up in excitement.

Uh oh, what happened to all the cakes?

What an odd bunch.
Prickles, Morris, Bugzy, Coco,
Lilly, and Nigel.
But Wiggleson loves them all.

They all love him. He is kind and
always makes them feel welcomed.
He would do anything for them.

Except for saving them cake! He is a pig, after all.

It's the thought that counts, right?

If you have enjoyed this book,
please leave a review on Amazon.
It has a significant impact on
independent creatives like myself.

Thank you so much!

Luna James

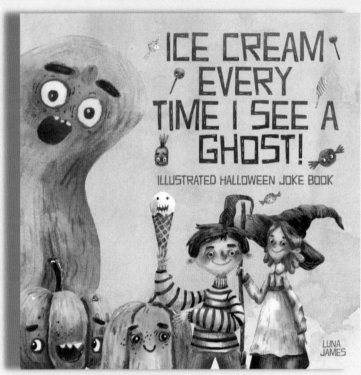

My other books are also available on Amazon.

Printed in Great Britain
by Amazon